The Legend of the
Flying
Dutchman

by Elizabeth Dale and Art Gus

W

The Legend of the Flying Dutchman

Contents

Chapter 1

How it all Began

I write this story for all who know me. I'm sorry that I ran away, but most of all, I am sorry that I joined *The Flying Dutchman*. You may be wondering where I am. This story tells you everything and why you must never look for me.

I will start my story exactly a year ago. I was fast asleep in my hammock, blissfully unaware of what was to come. Suddenly rough hands shook me. For a moment I didn't know where I was, until I saw Jason, the first mate, glaring at me.

And then I remembered exactly where I was –
on a ship sailing to the East Indies. I'd signed up as
a cabin boy to see the world. But so far, all I'd seen
were rough seas and each corner of the ship as
I'd scrubbed it with freezing water. Every muscle in
my body ached ...

"Come on, boy!" Jason cried. "Your watch started
two minutes ago."

"All right," I muttered, struggling to get out of
my hammock before he tipped me out. My watch
seemed to come sooner each day.

Yawning, I stumbled past sleeping crew members and made my way to the ladder that led to the deck. The boat was rocking so hard, that for every step forward, I went back three. Finally, I managed to reach the ladder. I climbed up, opened the hatch and stuck my head out.

SPLASH! A wave of ice-cold water hit me hard, cascading all over me, freezing me to the bone. At first, I wondered if it was the captain, thinking a bucket of cold water was an amusing way to make sure I was properly awake, but then ... SPLASH! There it was again. No, it wasn't a bucket of water. It was far, far worse. It was the sea. Huge waves were crashing over the side of the ship.

Chapter 2

Facing the Storm

It must be hard for you to imagine such a scene.

It was truly frightening, I can tell you.

I immediately took a step back down the ladder.

"What do you think you're doing?" a voice snarled.

I looked up. It was the captain. He was holding on

tightly to a rail, blown by the howling wind.

"It's not safe up there," I cried. "I might get washed overboard!"

The captain laughed nastily. "If you go back below deck," he sneered, "I'll make you wish you *had* been washed overboard. Start scrubbing those decks!"

Had he lost his mind? The sea was washing the decks for him! But one look at his face told me not to argue.

I clambered on to the deck, and clung to a post, looking around. The huge waves were grey and frightening, edged with white as they reared up. I managed to dodge the next wave as it crashed over the side. Then I slithered along the deck, sliding around as the ship rocked wildly.

I tried to tie myself down with a rope but my fingers were too numb. I looked around for help, but the rest of the crew were struggling to keep the ship on course.

"What are you doing?" yelled the captain to a crew member halfway up the main mast.
"Preparing to take down the sails," the sailor yelled.
"No ship of mine takes its sails down in a gale," the captain shouted. "It's our chance to go faster!"

I gasped and stared at my fellow sailors. We all knew it was madness to keep the sails up in such wild weather. I opened my mouth to protest, but before I could speak, Harry yelled, "Come here, Jack, quick, and help me tighten this sail!"

With difficulty, I scrambled over to him. "Best not to argue with the captain," Harry said, as I grabbed the rope beside him. I pulled on it hard, but the wind was tugging it even harder.

"This is ridiculous," muttered Jason, grabbing

the rope, too. "Keeping sails up like this is so risky.

They're likely to be ripped to shreds,

then we'll be lost. Pull, boy! Pull!"

I *was* pulling! I was pulling

as hard as I could!

Once we'd fastened that sail,

we moved on to another one.

Then another. We battled that

storm for two hours, and I was

exhausted. My elbows and knees

were cut and bruised, my hands

were red and raw and I was freezing cold.

"Right, lad!" Harry yelled. "You've done enough.

Come down for dinner." I didn't need telling twice.

I liked Harry. He was kind to me and gave me extra food. I squeezed in beside him and hungrily ate my salt beef and ships' biscuits.

"It's wild out there," I said. Everyone laughed. What had I said now?

"We can tell this is your first trip," said Harry. "You wait until we get to the Cape of Good Hope. This is a gentle breeze compared to the South African storms."

I shuddered. Surely it couldn't possibly get worse?

"The captain will have you working twice as hard, then," said Jason. "We won't even have time to eat."

I stared at him, horrified. He wasn't joking.

Chapter 3

Calm at Last

The storm continued for three days and nights. I went to sleep in cold, wet clothes and got up in them. And then on the fourth day, I woke to find the boat was strangely still.

When I went up on deck, I saw a calm, sparkling sea and a cloudless blue sky. It looked so beautiful. You'd have loved it if you could have seen it.

Harry smiled when he saw me.

"Look there, lad," he cried, pointing out to sea.

I shielded my eyes. At first I could see nothing.

Then I spotted a flash of grey amongst the waves.

"Dolphins!" Harry said, smiling. "We call them the sailors' friends. They watch out for us when we are at sea."

So beautiful and graceful, the dolphins leapt through the waves. It was a thrilling sight.

"Look sharp!" the captain yelled.

I turned quickly. He seemed angry – as always.

"Do you want any supper tonight? Get to work, boy! Polish the ship's bell until I can see my face in it."

"Yes, Captain," I said, rushing over to the bell.

Harry followed.

"Why is the captain always so cross and in a rush?" I asked him.

Harry sighed. "He wants to make as much money as he can," he said. "He has to feed us and pay our wages. Every day that we are at sea costs him more money. He wants to get back home with a ship full of cargo as quickly as possible."

"But won't he make lots of money from all the things we'll bring back?" I asked.

"Oh yes," said Harry, "the spices and silks we pick up from India and China are worth a fortune. But the captain is very greedy. Whatever he earns isn't enough for him."

Chapter 4

Danger Returns

The days that followed were some of my happiest on board ship. I saw dolphins, turtles and huge flying fish, and we sailed on as fast as our ship could go. Then everything changed.

As we passed the Cape of Good Hope, we ran into terrible, howling gales. And it was then I knew what rough weather really was. Dark grey clouds flew across the sky, bringing endless rain.

The angry wind screamed as it tore through the rigging, as though it was trying to rip the sails from the ship. But still the captain refused to haul them down. I was sure we would capsize then. But by some miracle we didn't.

Once past the Cape, everything was calm again. We sailed on to India and China to load up our cargo. What interesting ports we docked at. I gazed at mosques and temples, elephants and monkeys and people in exotic clothes, and I longed to leave the ship to explore. This was why I had come to sea. But the captain said there was too much work to allow time ashore.

My disappointment turned to terror when, laden with priceless goods, we sailed back past the Cape of Good Hope and were struck by a storm far worse than any we'd suffered before.

I had thought the winds had been noisy then, but now they were deafening. They whipped up waves higher even than our tallest mast. Everyone was called on deck to help sail our vessel as the waves grew ever larger, tossing our big ship about like it was a child's toy. But the captain just strode amongst us, swigging rum and insisting that we kept up every sail and rode out the storm.

"Please sir, put into port," begged Harry after we'd

been battered for hours.

"If we don't, we'll surely drown," I cried.

But the captain took another swig of rum

and simply yelled "Sail on!"

Bigger and bigger grew the waves that crashed

against the bow of the ship. Stronger and more

fiercely blew the gale. Desperately, we pleaded

with the captain again. But still he would not turn

back. Was he drunk or mad? Nobody knew.

The storm grew worse. Raging winds tore at

the sails and water poured over the sides, spilling

down into the hull.

Chapter 5

The Ship Speaks

We were in the most dangerous seas that any of the crew had ever seen. Huge waves now loomed above us on all sides. Even Jason, who always obeyed the captain's commands, realised that it was now time to stand up to him.

Like the rest of us, he knew we would sink unless we headed back to the safety of port. So, with Jason in the lead, we fought our way along the wave-lashed decks and on to the bridge to find the captain.

The captain was red-faced and wild-eyed as he turned to face us. Nervously, Jason yelled above the noise of the howling storm, telling him that we would no longer obey his command and we were turning back to port.

But the captain just laughed. Then he picked up Jason and threw him overboard into the churning seas to his certain, terrible death.

23

We were all horrified. Now, none of us would dare disobey the captain again. We turned to go, when suddenly, above the roar of the wild winds, we heard a strange, creaky voice. It seemed to be coming from the wooden deck and the masts themselves. It was the ship!

"Captain, what is your plan?" the ship creaked. "Do you wish to seek safety and shelter tonight?"

This was beyond anything I had ever imagined. How could a ship talk? But the captain laughed. "No!" he cried. "I'm not afraid of the storm. May I be cursed by God if I even try to seek shelter. I will not give in and go back. Even if it means I have to sail these seas until the Day of Judgement!"

The ship seemed to roar, and then the strange

creaky voice spoke again.

 "Foolish Captain!" it cried. "As you've dared

to defy God, you will never reach port.

You have brought death to your crew, and yourself.

But death will bring you no rest.

As ghosts, you will be condemned to sail

the oceans for eternity. And worse, you will bring

death to any who see your ghostly ship!"

We gasped. We didn't want to die.

But the captain simply laughed and cried,

"Amen to that!" and took another swig of rum.

Then a terrible shudder went through the ship.

The captain was wrong to laugh, very wrong.

Suddenly I felt the blood run cold in my veins.

Everyone around shivered, went pale and collapsed

on to the deck. But whilst our deaths were

mercifully quick, our afterlife is never-ending.

For we became ghosts.

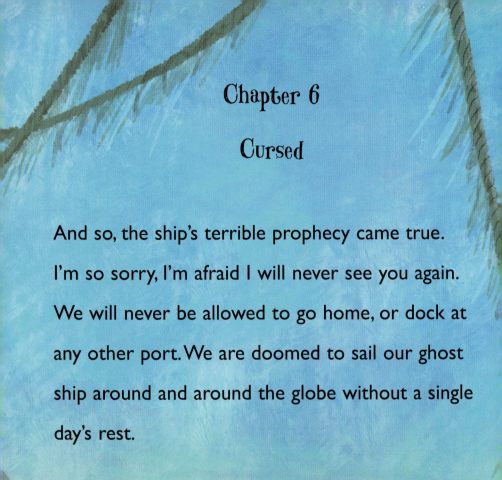

Chapter 6

Cursed

And so, the ship's terrible prophecy came true.

I'm so sorry, I'm afraid I will never see you again.

We will never be allowed to go home, or dock at

any other port. We are doomed to sail our ghost

ship around and around the globe without a single

day's rest.

It's very strange. I joined the *Flying Dutchman* to see the world – and I have. Yet, the rest of the prophecy has also come true. Death comes to every ship which sees us.

So please don't come looking for me. Just forgive me and know that I love you. And don't worry about me. I have good friends, especially Harry. We work hard but we also have fun, and we see beautiful dolphins galore. And at least as a ghost, I will never be hungry again.

Things to think about

1. Look at the opening of this story. How does the author get the reader interested in the story?
2. Look at the verbs the author uses when the captain speaks, for example, laughed nastily, sneered, yelled. What impression do they give of his character?
3. Do you think Jack is brave? Why or why not?
4. How do we know that Harry is kind to Jack?
5. At the end of the story, do you think Jack really enjoys his life on the ship?

Write it yourself

This story is based upon a legend, told from the point of view of a fictional character. Now try to write your own story, using a legend to base it on and telling it as if you were someone there at the time.

Plan your story before you begin to write it.

Start off with a story map:

• a beginning to introduce the characters and where and when your story is set (the setting);

• a problem which the main characters will need to fix in the story;

• an ending where the problems are resolved.

Get writing! Try to create an exciting opening sentence to grab your reader's attention.

Notes for parents and carers

Independent reading

The aim of independent reading is to read this book with ease. This series is designed to provide an opportunity for your child to read for pleasure and enjoyment. These notes are written for you to help your child make the most of this book.

About the book

This story is based on the legend of *The Flying Dutchman* and told from the point of view of Jack, a fictional cabin boy.

Before reading

Ask your child why they have selected this book. Look at the title and blurb together. What do they think it will be about? Do they think they will like it?

During reading

Encourage your child to read independently. If they get stuck on a longer word, remind them that they can find syllable chunks that can be sounded out from left to right. They can also read on in the sentence and think about what would make sense.

After reading

Support comprehension by talking about the story. What happened? Then help your child think about the messages in the book that go beyond the story, using the questions on the page opposite. Give your child a chance to respond to the story, asking:

Did you enjoy the story and why? Who was your favourite character? What was your favourite part? What did you expect to happen at the end?

Franklin Watts
First published in Great Britain in 2019
by The Watts Publishing Group

Series Editors: Jackie Hamley and Melanie Palmer
Series Advisors: Dr Sue Bodman and Glen Franklin
Series Designer: Peter Scoulding

A CIP catalogue record for this book is
available from the British Library.

ISBN 978 1 4451 6505 9 (hbk)
ISBN 978 1 4451 6506 6 (pbk)
ISBN 978 1 4451 6838 8 (library ebook)

Printed in China

Franklin Watts
An imprint of
Hachette Children's Group
Part of The Watts Publishing Group
Carmelite House
50 Victoria Embankment
London EC4Y 0DZ

An Hachette UK Company
www.hachette.co.uk

www.franklinwatts.co.uk

FSC
www.fsc.org
MIX
Paper from
responsible sources
FSC® C104740